For Mum and Dad, with love and gratitude,
and for my ever-creative muse
– P. B.

For Mini Minnie and
Minnie's mum and dad
– G. P.-R.

Text copyright © 2003 by Paul Bright
Illustrations copyright © 2003 by Guy Parker-Rees

First published in Great Britain in 2003 by Little Tiger Press

Library of Congress Cataloging-in-Publication Data available

ISBN 0-439-54512-9

10 9 8 7 6 5 4 3 2 1   03 04 05 06 07

Printed in Singapore
Reinforced binding for library use
First Scholastic edition, September 2003

QUIET!

By
Paul Bright

Illustrated by
Guy Parker-Rees

Orchard Books • **New York**
An Imprint of Scholastic Inc.

Deep, deep in the jungle,
chimps were chattering,

frogs were croaking,

birds were chirping,

and a million insects were humming and buzzing. That's a lot of noise!

It was time for
Baby Leo to take his morning nap.
"He'll never get to sleep with all this noise,"
said Mama Lion to Leo's father.
"Isn't there something you can do?"

"Do?" said Papa Lion. "Do?
I am king of all the animals. Of course
there is something I can do!"
He stood up tall, puffed out his
huge chest, and roared . . .

And so, Baby Leo fell asleep. Then Papa Lion
whispered softly, but clearly so that all
the creatures could hear him:

"If any of you makes a noise,
and wakes up Leo, I will gobble you up."

And all was quiet in the jungle.
Quiet as the morning mist.
Quiet as the opening flowers.
Quiet as a baby sleeping.
Suddenly . . .

Cawing and crowing, squeaking and squawking.
Beaks pecking and claws scratching.
Two parrots were arguing in the bushes!

"**Quiet!**" said Papa Lion, as loud as he dared,
in case Baby Leo was still sleeping.
"It's all right," said Mama Lion. "Leo's fast asleep."
"Oh well," said Papa Lion. "But I could have used a snack."

Once again, all was quiet in the jungle.
Quiet as the trees growing toward the sky.
Quiet as the leaves reaching toward the light.
Quiet as a baby sleeping. Suddenly . . .

Chuckling
and chortling,

sniggering
and snickering.

The hyena was laughing.
Laughing like hyenas do.

But nobody knew what was so funny.

"**Quiet!**" said Papa Lion, as loud as he dared,
in case his son was still sleeping.
"It's all right," said Mama Lion. "He's still asleep."
"Oh, well," said Papa Lion. "But I am getting hungry."

Then all was quiet in the jungle.
Quiet as the calm after a storm.
Quiet as sunshine after rain.
Quiet as a baby sleeping. Suddenly . . .

Howling and hooting, screeching and chattering.
Swinging and swooping. A family of monkeys was
leaping through the trees!

"Quiet!" said Papa Lion, as loud as he dared,
just in case Leo was still sleeping.
"It's all right," said Mama Lion. "Leo's asleep."
"Oh, well," said Papa Lion. "But now I'm *very* hungry."

It was the middle of the day
and the jungle was hot and humid.
The animals crept into the shade
of the trees, drowsy and dozing.

And all was quiet in the jungle.
Quiet as the blazing sun.
Quiet as the shadows underneath the trees.
Quiet as a baby sleeping. Suddenly . . .

Splashing and squelching.

Oohing and aahing.

A hippopotamus was
yawning in the cool, muddy
shallows of the river.

"**Quiet!**" said Papa Lion, as loud as he dared,
in case the baby lion was still sleeping.
"It's all right," said Mama Lion. "Leo's fast asleep."
"Humph!" said Papa Lion.
"I guess my eyes are bigger than my belly."

But Papa Lion rubbed his tummy and began to think,
"I do wish someone would make just a little
more noise and wake up Baby Leo.
Just for a minute."

Yet all remained quiet in the jungle.
Quiet as a fish swimming in the river.
Quiet as a bird soaring in the sky.
Quiet as a baby sleeping. Suddenly . . .

A rumbling and growling,
a groaning and moaning, a gurgling and burbling.
A noise like nothing ever heard before!

Loud as thunder.
Loud as a banging drum.
Loud as a baby crying!

"It's me," said Papa Lion, meekly.
"My stomach is rumbling.
Because I'm so hungry!"